FLUTES AND CYMBALS

ALSO BY LEONARD CLARK

Drums and Trumpets

POETRY FOR THE YOUNGEST

Flutes and Cymbals

POETRY FOR THE YOUNG

SELECTED BY

LEONARD CLARK

AND ILLUSTRATED BY

SHIRLEY HUGHES

THE BODLEY HEAD

LONDON SYDNEY

TORONTO

Illustrations © The Bodley Head Ltd 1968
ISBN 0 370 01090 6
Printed Offset Litho and bound in Great Britain for
The Bodley Head Ltd
9 Bow Street, London WC2E 7AL
by Cox & Wyman Ltd, Fakenham
Set in Monotype Baskerville
First published 1968
Reprinted 1975

Contents

Contents

Contents

Contents

Introduction

The poems in a previous anthology, *Drums and Trumpets*, were chosen for the youngest, 'for the child looking at the world, and seeing "all that therein is" for the first time'. The poems in the present collection are intended for slightly older children, many of whom will be well able to read for themselves, with confidence and fuller understanding. For this reason there are no nursery rhymes included, but many poems, and extracts of longer poems, which are more fitting to the age and experience of these older children. All the same, *Flutes and Cymbals* and *Drums and Trumpets* should be regarded as companion volumes since they both contain a wide range of poems by past and present poets which are not only suitable in themselves for young children but may also serve as an introduction to a far wider range of poetry at a later stage of development. This is particularly true of some of the more experimental and complex poetry of our own day. There is, alas, not a great deal of the more fashionable verse of today which appears to be very suitable for young children, not so much, perhaps, because of the nature of its content as the difficulty of its language. If there were such poems some of them would have been included here. There are also not many poets of high order who are writing specifically for the young in the same way as in previous generations, Christina Rossetti, R. L. Stevenson, Rudyard Kipling and Walter de la Mare did, to name but four. Not that there is any special poetry for the young, only good poetry which is appropriate to their stage of intellectual and imaginative growth.

Flutes and Cymbals, as was the case with *Drums and Trumpets*, is divided into sections and based on a number of contrasting themes which are the concern of these older children. It is realised that such themes are entirely arbitrary. The poems could be arranged in some other pattern, but they do, at least, allow for convenient breaks and should be considered as a kind of framework for the whole book. As in all anthologies the choices which have been made for each section are entirely personal. Some pieces which frequently occur in other anthologies have been deliberately

[9]

excluded and others included which may not be so familiar. But, all in all, the poems and extracts do represent a generous cross-section of poetry, so that any child who is on familiar terms with all of them would have a rich store of poetry to draw upon. The general aim has been to provide sensation but to avoid sensationalism, sentiment but not sentimentality, toughness but not violence and horror, genuine poetry rather than poetic propaganda. All these more mature aspects of life and poetry can be reserved for later years.

Many of these older children will already have enjoyed an experience of poetry which, if fortunate, they will have received at the hands of a sympathetic and informed adult, within the family circle, or at school. And many of them, too, with their added years will know more about the world around them—its people, creatures, happenings, scenery and seasons. But they will still be exploring and discovering, like the boy in W. J. Turner's poem, *Romance*, who was carried away by Chimborazo, Cotopaxi and shining Popocatapetl, they will echo Bunyan's words and 'labour night and day to be a pilgrim', and with growing awareness and sharpened feelings be acutely moved by the cruel treatment of John Clare's badger and W. H. Davies's sheep who were transported from Baltimore to Glasgow. And, on the other hand, many of them will be lost in wonder at the dignity of Shakespeare's horse and the apparent mystery of James Merrick's chameleon. It is at this stage, too, that stories, both of today and of the long ago, make their greatest impact so, in this book, these children can ride together with the Christian knights as conjured up by William Morris, have a small peep at what happened on that bloody occasion at Flodden in the words of Scott, watch with John Squire and that solitary Indian 'Columbus's doom-burdened caravels slant to the shore', die gloriously with Moore's minstrel boy, admire passionately the dog in Wordsworth's *Fidelity*. Or, on a happier plane, they can make the acquaintance of *Meg Merrilies* as Keats saw her, face to face, or of Whitman's ship, 'rusting, mouldering'.

It is during these later years of childhood that feelings are at their strongest and most extreme, when love, sorrow, joy, tenderness, and frustration matter so much, when so much is accepted for what it is, when so many questions are asked, when there is so much to be curious about. There is much to discuss about that unfortunate Mary who was drowned on the sands of Dee, as well as about the old manor farm which Edward Thomas came upon one Sunday afternoon in late winter. But, above all, this is the time in life when affection and security matter more than anything else because these are the progenitors of the happiness which will never again be so innocent and complete.

Several extracts from longer poems have been included and there will certainly be some adult readers who may object to the use of such extracts on the grounds that the whole poem should be presented in every case. But for young children such niceties of scholarship do not always apply. These children are like honey bees who sip where they will. They will have the whole of life to return to the longer poems in their entirety. Provided that the extracts are complete in themselves, do not falsify the intent of the whole poem, and are of sufficient interest as extracts, little harm will be done. In any case, the poet's original words remain. In some cases the whole poem may just not be good enough to present as a whole and therefore hardly worth bothering about, even at a much later stage.

The book should be read through first of all from cover to cover, so that its shape and tone may be appreciated, always remembering that it is the compilation of a single mind and heart, of one individual with his own likes and dislikes and his own strong beliefs about what is likely to appeal to the greatest number of children. The book, then, should be regarded as a whole as well as a collection of single poems and extracts arranged in a certain order.

Then come back to the individual poems which have impressed most of all at the first reading. Read and study these more carefully, think about them, ask questions about them. For instance, do you agree with what D. H. Lawrence said about people talking? Do you prefer, with Thomas Moult, the country to the town? Do you know of other hills like John Dyer's 18th century Grongar? What does Clifford Dyment mean when he calls winter the 'chastiser of the free'? Why did Walter de la Mare call his poem about the Siamese cat, *Double Dutch?* Then, if you find you enjoy the poem by a particular writer, discover other poems of his and copy them out in a notebook, thus making what will become the best anthology of all—your own. You will certainly find much to entertain and challenge you in the poems by Lawrence, Clare, Tennyson and Blake, in the translations from Chinese poetry, in ballads, and in the modern renderings of medieval poems. That prolific author 'Anon' will also have much to reveal to you.

Another way of adding to your enjoyment is to find more poems which you think would not be out of place in each of the sections. English poetry is well blessed, for instance, with poems about the countryside, birds and beasts, the past, other countries, ordinary people. In this way you can extend the horizons of your experience.

Learn some of the poems by heart. In this way they will not only give you a great deal of present satisfaction but also become your firm and lasting friends so that you will be able to savour them in the years to come. They will say more to you as you grow older and help to fill your mind with thoughts which are neither trivial, coy, nor counterfeit. A head that is full of poems is not unlike a ragbag—ever a source of pleasure.

Try and write your own poems, not only poems which could find a place in some of the sections in *Flutes and Cymbals*, but also poems which are entirely your own, about your own experiences

Introduction

as you have known them at first hand. Some of the poems in this book may help to start you off. Poets, past and present, will have much to tell you about your own feelings and how best to express them.

Long then may the poems in this book be enjoyed, and by generations of children who are discovering for themselves what poetry can mean to them in all its truth and beauty of language and content. Life has its flutes as well as its cymbals, the soft notes as well as the loud clashes.

Leonard Clark

THE LOTUS-EATERS

There is sweet music here that softer falls
Than petals from blown roses on the grass,
Or night-dews on still waters between walls
Of shadowy granite, in a gleaming pass;
Music that gentlier on the spirit lies
Than tired eyelids upon tired eyes;

from *The Lotus-Eaters*, Alfred, Lord Tennyson

ROMANCE

When I was but thirteen or so
    I went into a golden land,
Chimborazo, Cotopaxi
    Took me by the hand.

My father died, my brother too,
    They passed like fleeting dreams.
I stood where Popocatapetl
    In the sunlight gleams.

I dimly heard the Master's voice
    And the boys' far-off play,
Chimborazo, Cotopaxi
    Had stolen me away.

I walked in a great golden dream
    To and fro from school—
Shining Popocatapetl
    The dusty streets did rule.

I walked home with a gold dark boy
    And never a word I'd say,
Chimborazo, Cotopaxi
    Had taken my speech away:

I gazed entranced upon his face
    Fairer than any flower—
O shining Popocatapetl,
    It was thy magic hour:

The houses, people, traffic, seemed
    Thin fading dreams by day,
Chimborazo, Cotopaxi
    They had stolen my soul away!

W. J. Turner

MUSIC

Orpheus with his lute made trees,
    And the mountain-tops that freeze,
Bow themselves when he did sing.
    To his music plants and flowers
Ever sprung: as sun and showers
    There had made a lasting spring.
Everything that heard him play,
    Even the billows of the sea,
Hung their heads, and then lay by.
    In sweet music is such art,
Killing care and grief of heart
    Fall asleep, or, hearing, die.

John Fletcher

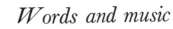

SPANISH FOLK SONG

In a pitcher I have
   My songs in store.
When I wish I uncork it,
   And out they pour.

Of the dust of the earth
   Can I make songs.
One is scarcely over
   A new one comes.

My body is like a wasp-nest,
   Crowded with songs,
Each to come out so eager
   They come in throngs.

Translated by S. De Madariaga

THE HILL OF VISION

Sing to me once again before I go from here . . .

The joyful song that welcomes in the spring,
The tender mating song so bravely shy,
The song that builds the nest, the merry ring
When the long wait is ended and ye bring
The young birds out and teach them how to fly:
Sing to me of the beechnuts on the ground,
And of the first wild flight at early dawn,
And of the store of berries someone found
And hid away until ye gathered round
And ate them while he shrieked upon the lawn:
Sing of the swinging nest upon the tree,
And of your mates who call and hide away,
And of the sun that shines exceedingly,
And of the leaves that dance, and all the glee
And rapture that begins at break of day . . .

from *The Hill of Vision*, James Stephens

A COUNTING-OUT
RHYME

Intery, mintery, cutery-corn,
Apple seed and apple thorn;
Wine, brier, limber-lock,
Five geese in a flock,
Sit and sing by a spring,
O-U-T, and in again.

Anon.

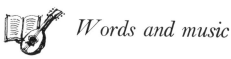

INTRODUCTION

Piping down the valleys wild,
Piping songs of pleasant glee,
On a cloud I saw a child,
And he laughing said to me:

"Pipe a song about a Lamb!"
So I piped with merry cheer.
"Piper, pipe that song again;"
So I piped: he wept to hear.

"Drop thy pipe, thy happy pipe;
Sing thy songs of happy cheer;"
So I sang the same again,
While he wept with joy to hear.

"Piper, sit thee down and write
In a book, that all may read."
So he vanished from my sight,
And I plucked a hollow reed,

And I made a rural pen,
And I stained the water clear,
And I wrote my happy songs
Every child may joy to hear.

from Songs of Innocence, William Blake

TALK

I wish people, when you sit near them,
wouldn't think it necessary to make conversation
and send thin draughts of words
blowing down your neck and your ears
and giving you a cold in your inside.

D. H. Lawrence

THE PILGRIM

Who would true valour see,
Let him come hither;
One here will constant be,
Come wind come weather.
There's no discouragement
Shall make him once relent
His first avowed intent
To be a Pilgrim.

Who so beset him round
With dismal stories
Do but themselves confound;
His strength the more is.
No lion can him fright,
He'll with a giant fight;
But he will have a right
To be a Pilgrim.

Hobgoblin nor foul fiend
Can daunt his spirit:
He knows he at the end
Shall life inherit.
Then fancies fly away,
He'll fear not what men say,
He'll labour night and day
To be a Pilgrim.

John Bunyan

TOWN AND COUNTRY

"My child, the town's a fine place,
With glittering streets of gold."
I'd sooner have the buttercups—
All my two hands can hold.

"Why, child, the town's a bright place,
With gay lights all the way."
I've heard they grudge the sunshine,
And even the light of day.

"No no, the town's a good place,
With churches and proud towers."
But won't they steal my roses
And give me paper flowers?

"O come, the town's a kind place
With pretty silks and silver, lass."
I'd rather have the silken cows
And the silver dew in the grass!

Thomas Moult

AFTERNOON
ON A HILL

I will be the gladdest thing
   Under the sun!
I will touch a hundred flowers
   And not pick one.

I will look at cliffs and clouds
   With quiet eyes,
Watch the wind bow down the grass
   And the grass rise.

And when lights begin to show
   Up from the town,
I will mark which must be mine,
   And then start down!

              Edna St. Vincent Millay

CHAUCER'S THAMES

Forget six counties overhung with smoke,
Forget the snorting steam and piston stroke,
Forget the spreading of the hideous town;
Think rather of the pack-horse on the down,
And dream of London, small and white and clean,
The clear Thames bordered by its gardens green;
Think, that below bridge, the green lapping waves
Smite some few keels that bear Levantine staves,
Cut from the yew-wood on the burnt-up hill,
And pointed jars that Greek hands toiled to fill,
And treasured scanty spice from some far sea,
Florence gold cloth, and Ypres napery,
And cloth of Bruges, and hogshead of Guienne;

from *Chaucer's Thames*, William Morris

GRONGAR HILL

Old castles on the cliff arise,
Proudly towering in the skies.
Rushing from the woods, the spires
Seem from hence ascending fires.

Below me, trees unnumbered rise,
Beautiful in various dyes:
The gloomy pine, the poplar blue,
The yellow beech, the sable yew,
The slender fir that taper grows,
The sturdy oak with broad-spread boughs.

. . . .

from *Grongar Hill*, John Dyer

THE CRY OF THE CHILDREN

" . . . . .

For, all day, we drag our burden tiring
   Through the coal-dark, underground;
Or, all day, we drive the wheels of iron
   In the factories, round and round.

"For all day the wheels are droning, turning;
   Their wind comes in our faces,
Till our hearts turn, our heads with pulses burning,
   And the walls turn in their places;
Turns the sky in the high window, blank and reeling,
   Turns the long light that drops adown the wall,
Turn the black flies that crawl along the ceiling:
   All are turning, all the day, and we with all,
And all the day, the iron wheels are droning,
   And sometimes we could pray,
'O ye wheels' (breaking out in a mad moaning)
   'Stop! be silent for to-day!'"

from *The Cry of the Children*, Elizabeth Barrett Browning

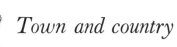

EVENING OVER
THE FOREST

Watch.
  What is it you see?

The stark bough of an oak.
Beyond it the evening sky.
Clear, clear the evening sky
And green like a green pearl.

Did you hear?
What did you hear?

The harsh cry of a bird,
Beyond the evening sky.
Still, still the evening sky
And green like a green pearl.

Oh, search.
What is it you see?

Fiery snowy little cloud
Sailing to sleep in the sky.
Dim, dim the evening sky
Like a deep green pearl.

Come away.
Come away.

Beatrice Mayor

Up at Piccadilly, o!
  The coachman takes his stand,
And when he meets a pretty girl,
  He takes her by the hand.
    Whip away for ever, o!
    Drive away so clever, o!
    All the way to Bristol, o!
  He drives her four-in-hand.

Anon.

SOWING

It was a perfect day
For sowing: just
As sweet and dry was the ground
As tobacco-dust.

I tasted deep the hour
Between the far
Owl's chuckling first soft cry
And the first star.

A long stretched hour it was;
Nothing undone
Remained; the early seeds
All safely sown.

And now, hark at the rain,
Windless and light,
Half a kiss, half a tear,
Saying good-night.

Edward Thomas

EVENING

The sun is set; the swallows are asleep;
   The bats are flitting fast in the grey air;
The slow soft toads out of dim corners creep,
   And evening's breath, wandering here and there
Over the quivering surface of the stream,
Wakes not one ripple from its summer dream.

There is no dew on the dry grass tonight,
   Nor damp within the shadow of the trees;
The wind is intermitting, dry, and light;
   And in the inconstant motion of the breeze
The dust and straws are driven up and down,
And whirled about the pavement of the town.

from *Evening*, P. B. Shelley

BELEAGUERED CITIES

Build your houses, build your houses, build your slums,
   Drive your drains where once the rabbits used to lurk,
Let there be no song there save the wind that hums
   Through the idle wires while dumb men tramp to work,
   Tramp to their idle work.
Silent the siege; none notes it; yet one day
Men from your walls shall watch the woods once more
   Close round their prey.
Build, build the ramparts of your giant-town;
Yet they shall crumble to the dust before
   The battering thistle-down.

from *Beleaguered Cities*, F. L. Lucas

WINTER
THE HUNTSMAN

Through his iron glades
Rides Winter the Huntsman.
All colour fades
As his horn is heard sighing.

Far through the forest
His wild hooves crash and thunder
Till many a mighty branch
Is torn asunder.

And the red reynard creeps
To his hole near the river,
The copper leaves fall
And the bare trees shiver.

As night creeps from the ground,
Hides each tree from its brother,
And each dying sound
Reveals yet another.

Is it Winter the Huntsman
Who gallops through his iron glades,
Cracking his cruel whip
To the gathering shades?

Osbert Sitwell

COLD BLOWS THE WIND

Loud rairs the blast amang the woods,
   The branches tirling barely,
Amang the chimley taps it thuds,
   And frost is nippin sairly.
Now up in the morning's no' for me,
   Up in the morning early;
To sit a' the night I'd rather agree,
   Than rise in the morning early.

from *Cold Blows the Wind*, John Hamilton

SNOW HARVEST

The moon that now and then last night
Glanced between clouds in flight
Saw the white harvest that spread over
The stubble fields and even roots and clover.

It climbed the hedges, overflowed
And trespassed on the road,
Weighed down fruit-trees and when winds woke
From white-thatched roofs rose in a silver smoke.

How busy is the world to-day!
Sun reaps, rills bear away
The lovely harvest of the snow
While bushes weep loud tears to see it go.

Andrew Young

TARDY SPRING

For iron Winter held her firm;
Across her sky he laid his hand;
And bird he starved, he stiffened worm;
A sightless heaven, a shaven land . . .
Now the North wind ceases,
The warm South-west awakes,
The heavens are out in fleeces,
And earth's green banner shakes.

from *Tardy Spring*, George Meredith

OLD DAN'L

Out of his cottage to the sun
Bent double comes old Dan'l,
His chest all over cotton wool,
His back all over flannel.

"Winter will finish him," they've said
Each winter now for ten:
But come the first warm day of Spring
Old Dan'l's out again.

L. A. G. Strong

THE YOUTHFUL SPRING

Now that the Winter's gone, the earth has lost
Her snow-white robes, and now no more the frost
Candies the grass, or calls an icy cream
Upon the silver lake, or crystal stream;

But the warm sun thaws the benumb'd earth,
And makes it tender; gives a second birth
To the dead swallow; wakes in hollow tree
The drowsy cuckoo, and the humble bee:

Now do a choir of chirping minstrels bring
In triumph to the world the youthful Spring.

Thomas Carew

ON A MAY MORNING

Now the bright morning-star, day's harbinger,
Comes dancing from the east, and leads with her
The flowery May, who from her green lap throws
The yellow cowslip and the pale primrose.
 Hail, bounteous May, that dost inspire
 Mirth and youth and warm desire!
 Woods and groves are of thy dressing,
 Hill and dale doth boast thy blessing:
Thus we salute thee with our early song,
And welcome thee, and wish thee long.

from On a May Morning, John Milton

THE SADDEST NOISE,
THE SWEETEST NOISE

The saddest noise, the sweetest noise,
The maddest noise that grows,
The birds, they make it in the spring,
At night's delicious close

Between the March and April line,
That magical frontier
Beyond which summer hesitates,
Almost too heavenly near.

from *The Saddest Noise, the Sweetest Noise*, Emily Dickinson

SUMMER

A butterfly,
Black and scarlet,
Spotted with white,
Fans its wings
Over a privet flower.

A thousand crimson foxgloves,
Tall bloody pikes,
Stand motionless in the gravel quarry;
The wind runs over them.

A rose film over a pale sky
Fantastically cut by dark chimneys;
Candles winking in the windows
Across an old garden city.

Richard Aldington

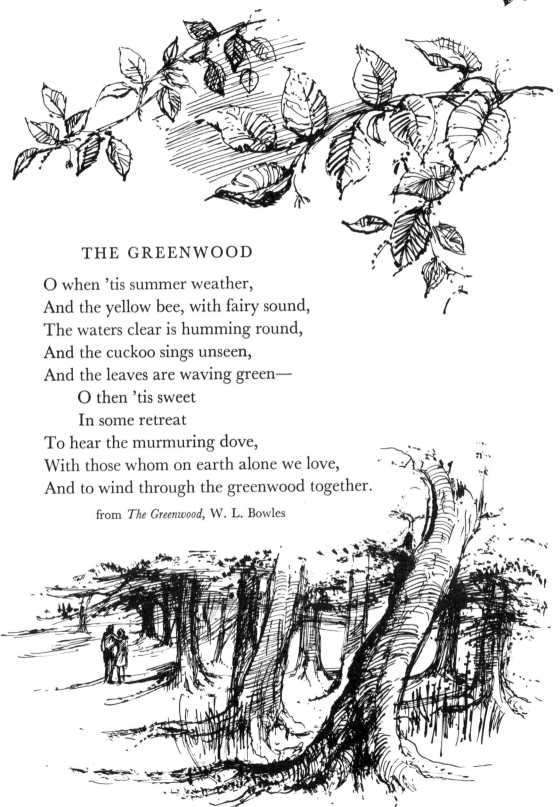

THE GREENWOOD

O when 'tis summer weather,
And the yellow bee, with fairy sound,
The waters clear is humming round,
And the cuckoo sings unseen,
And the leaves are waving green—
    O then 'tis sweet
    In some retreat
To hear the murmuring dove,
With those whom on earth alone we love,
And to wind through the greenwood together.

       from *The Greenwood*, W. L. Bowles

THE SHOWER

. . . . . .

Many fair ev'nings, many flow'rs
Sweetened with rich and gentle showers,
Have I enjoyed, and down have run
Many a fine and shining sun;
But never, till this happy hour,
Was blest with such an evening-shower!

from *The Shower*, Henry Vaughan

Lo! sweeten'd with the summer light,
The full juiced apple, waxing over-mellow,
Drops in a silent autumn night.

from *Choric Song*, Alfred, Lord Tennyson

TO AUTUMN

. . . . . .

Where are the songs of Spring? Ay, where are they?
 Think not of them, thou hast thy music too,
While barred clouds bloom the soft-dying day,
 And touch the stubble-plains with rosy hue;
Then in a wailful choir the small gnats mourn
 Among the river sallows, borne aloft
  Or sinking as the light wind lives or dies;
And full-grown lambs loud bleat from hilly bourn;
 Hedge-crickets sing; and now with treble soft
 The red-breast whistles from a garden-croft,
  And gathering swallows twitter in the skies.

from *To Autumn*, John Keats

AUTUMN

I love the fitful gust that shakes
The casement all the day,
And from the glossy elm-tree takes
The faded leaves away,
Twirling them by the window pane
With thousand others down the lane.

I love to see the shaking twig
Dance till the shut of eve,
The sparrow on the cottage rig,
Whose chirp would make believe
That Spring was just now flirting by
In Summer's lap with flowers to lie.

I love to see the cottage smoke
Curl upwards through the trees,
The pigeons nestled round the cote
On November days like these:
The cock upon the dunghill crowing,
The mill-sails on the heath a-going.

The feather from the raven's breast
Falls on the stubble lea,
The acorns near the old crow's nest
Fall pattering down the tree:
The grunting pigs that wait for all,
Scramble and hurry where they fall.

John Clare

JARDINS SOUS LA PLUIE

Tenderly, gently, the soft rain
fell on the garden, and it was nearing night;
only a little grey light
filtered through the west's clouded window-pane.

Tenderly, gently, the soft rain, dripping
with a hushed shimmer of sound,
fell from leaf to leaf, and ran slipping
down wet tree-trunks to the ground.

from *Jardins sous la Pluie*, John Redwood-Anderson

AND IT WAS
WINDY WEATHER

Now the winds are riding by;
Clouds are galloping the sky;

Bush and tree are lashing bare,
Savage boughs on savage air;

Crying, as they lash and sway,
—Pull the roots out of the clay!

Lift away: away:
Away!

Leave security, and speed
From the root, the mud, the mead!

Into sea and air, we go!
To chase the gull, the moon!—and know,

—Flying high!
Flying high!—

All the freedom of the sky!
All the freedom of the sky!

James Stephens

DOVER BEACH

The sea is calm to-night.
The tide is full, the moon lies fair
Upon the Straits—on the French coast, the light
Gleams, and is gone: the cliffs of England stand,
Glimmering and vast, out in the tranquil bay.

Come to the window, sweet is the night air!
Only, from the long line of spray
Where the sea meets the moon-blanched sand,
Listen! you hear the grating roar
Of pebbles which the waves suck back, and fling,
At their return, up the high strand,
Begin, and cease, and then again begin,

. . . . . .

from *Dover Beach*, Matthew Arnold

NOAH

When old Noah stared across the floods,
Sky and water melted into one
Looking-glass of shifting tides and sun.

Mountain-tops were few: the ship was foul:
All the morn old Noah marvelled greatly
At this weltering world that shone so stately,
Drowning deep the rivers and the plains.
Through the stillness came a rippling breeze;
Noah sighed, remembering the green trees.

Clear along the morning stooped a bird, —
Lit beside him with a blossomed sprig.
Earth was saved; and Noah danced a jig.

Siegfried Sassoon

THE WIND AND THE RAIN

Roman, Roman, what do you here?
Your great Wall is fallen this many a year—
Fallen, fallen, the Roman Wall;
And green grow the bent and the moss over all.

The wind and the rain have tumbled down
What the foemen left of tower and town.
Well and truly you builded your Wall,
But the wind and the rain are the masters of all:

Bravely you builded: but all in vain
Man builds against the wind and the rain:
The raking wind and the seeping rain,
Whatever man builds, unbuild again.
Man builds in vain, for the wind and the wet,
The water that saps and the airs that fret,
His pride of towers will overset.

Man builds: but all must fall as the Wall
You builded, O Roman, to breast the squall:
The wide-flung ramparts and cities tall
Must fall as the Wall—yea, all must fall
And tempest ride over the ruins of all:
For the wind and the rain are the masters of all.

W. W. Gibson

THE BROOK

I come from haunts of coot and hern,
  I make a sudden sally,
And sparkle out among the fern,
  To bicker down a valley.

By thirty hills I hurry down,
  Or slip between the ridges,
By twenty thorps, a little town,
  And half a hundred bridges.

Till last by Philip's farm I flow
  To join the brimming river,
For men may come and men may go,
  But I go on for ever.

I chatter over stony ways,
  In little sharps and trebles,
I bubble into eddying bays,
  I babble on the pebbles.

With many a curve my banks I fret
  By many a field and fallow,
And many a fairy foreland set
  With willow-seed and mallow.

I chatter, chatter, as I flow
   To join the brimming river,
For men may come and men may go,
   But I go on for ever.

I wind about, and in and out,
   With here a blossom sailing,
And here and there a lusty trout,
   And here and there a grayling,

And here and there a foaming flake
   Upon me, as I travel
With many a silvery waterbreak
   Above the golden gravel,

And draw them all along, and flow
   To join the brimming river,
For men may come and men may go,
   But I go on for ever.

I steal by lawns and grassy plots,
   I slide by hazel covers;
I move the sweet forget-me-nots
   That grow for happy lovers.

I slip, I slide, I gloom, I glance,
   Among my skimming swallows;
I make the netted sunbeam dance
   Against my sandy shallows.

I murmur under moon and stars
   In brambly wildernesses;
I linger by my shingly bars;
   I loiter round my cresses;

And out again I curve and flow
   To join the brimming river,
For men may come and men may go,
   But I go on for ever.

              Alfred, Lord Tennyson

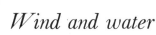

A WET SHEET AND
A FLOWING SEA

A wet sheet and a flowing sea,
 A wind that follows fast,
And fills the white and rustling sail,
 And bends the gallant mast;
And bends the gallant mast, my boys,
 While, like the eagle free,
Away the good ship flies, and leaves
 Old England on the lee.

Oh for a soft and gentle wind!
 I heard a fair one cry;
But give to me the snorting breeze,
 And white waves heaving high;
And white waves heaving high, my boys,
 The good ship tight and free—
The world of waters is our home,
 And merry men are we.

There's tempest in yon hornèd moon,
    And lightning in yon cloud:
And hark the music, mariners!
    The wind is piping loud;
The wind is piping loud, my boys,
    The lightning flashing free,
While the hollow oak our palace is,
    Our heritage the sea.

        Allan Cunningham

THE POOL IN THE ROCK

In this water, clear as air,
Lurks a lobster in its lair.
Rock-bound weed sways out and in,
Coral-red, and bottle-green.
Wondrous pale anemones
Stir like flowers in a breeze:
Fluted scallop, whelk in shell,
And the prowling mackerel.
Winged with snow the sea-mews ride
The brine-keen wind; and far and wide
Sounds on the hollow thunder of the tide.

        Walter de la Mare

TRADE WINDS

In the harbour, in the island, in the Spanish Seas,
Are the tiny white houses and the orange-trees,
And day-long, night-long, the cool and pleasant breeze
    Of the steady Trade Winds blowing.

There is the red wine, the nutty Spanish ale,
The shuffle of the dancers, the old salt's tale,
The squeaking fiddle, and the soughing in the sail
    Of the steady Trade Winds blowing.

And o' nights there's fire-flies and the yellow moon,
In the ghostly palm-trees the sleepy tune
Of the quiet voice calling me, the long low croon
    Of the steady Trade Winds blowing.

John Masefield

CAMBRIDGE

I ran out in the morning, when the air was clean and new,
And all the grass was glittering and grey with autumn dew;
I ran out to an apple-tree and pulled an apple down,
And all the bells were ringing in the old grey town.

Down in the town off the bridges and the grass
They are sweeping up the leaves to let the people pass—
Sweeping up the old leaves, golden-reds and browns,
Whilst the men go to lecture with the wind in their gowns.

Frances Cornford

THE MANOR FARM

The rock-like mud unfroze a little and rills
Ran and sparkled down each side of the road
Under the catkins wagging in the hedge.
But earth would have her sleep out, spite of the sun,
Nor did I value that thin gilding beam
More than a pretty February thing
Till I came down to the old Manor Farm,
And church and yew-tree opposite, in age
Its equals and in size. The church and yew
And farmhouse slept in a Sunday silentness.
The air raised not a straw. The steep farm roof,
With tiles duskily glowing, entertained
The mid-day sun; and up and down the roof
White pigeons nestled. There was no sound but one.
Three cart-horses were looking over a gate
Drowsily through their forelocks, swishing their tails
Against a fly, a solitary fly.

from *The Manor Farm*, Edward Thomas

WANDER-THIRST

Yonder the long horizon lies, and there by night and day
The old ships draw to home again, the young ships sail away;
And come I may, but go I must, and, if men ask you why,
You may put the blame on the stars and the sun and the
white road and the sky.

from *Wander-Thirst*, Gerald Gould

REQUIEM

Under the wide and starry sky
Dig the grave and let me lie.
Glad did I live and gladly die,
And I laid me down with a will.

This be the verse you grave for me:
Here he lies where he longed to be:
Home is the sailor, home from sea,
And the hunter home from the hill.

Robert Louis Stevenson

NURSE'S SONG

When the voices of children are heard on the green,
And laughing is heard on the hill,
My heart is at rest within my breast,
And everything else is still.

"Then come home, my children, the sun is gone down,
And the dews of night arise;
Come, come, leave off play, and let us away
Till the morning appears in the skies."

"No, no, let us play, for it is yet day,
And we cannot go to sleep;
Besides, in the sky the little birds fly,
And the hills are all covered with sheep."

"Well, well, go and play till the light fades away,
And then go home to bed."
The little ones leaped and shouted and laughed
And all the hills echoèd.

William Blake

WHO'S IN

"The door is shut fast
And everyone's out."
But people don't know
What they're talking about!
Says the fly on the wall,
And the flame on the coals
And the dog on his rug
And the mice in their holes,
And the kitten curled up,
And the spiders that spin—
"What, everyone's out?
Why, everyone's in!"

Elizabeth Fleming

MY HEART'S IN THE HIGHLANDS

My heart's in the Highlands, my heart is not here;
My heart's in the Highlands, a-chasing the deer;
Chasing the wild deer, and following the roe,
My heart's in the Highlands, wherever I go.
Farewell to the Highlands, farewell to the North,
The birth-place of valour, the country of worth;
Wherever I wander, wherever I rove,
The hills of the Highlands for ever I love.

Farewell to the mountains high cover'd with snow;
Farewell to the straths and green valleys below;
Farewell to the forests and wild-hanging woods;
Farewell to the torrents and loud pouring floods.
My heart's in the Highlands, my heart is not here;
My heart's in the Highlands a-chasing the deer;
Chasing the wild deer and following the roe,
My heart's in the Highlands wherever I go.

Robert Burns

THE WINTER TREES

Against the evening sky the trees are black,
Iron themselves against the iron rails;
The hurrying crowds seek cinemas or homes,
A cosy hour where warmth will mock the wind.
They do not look at trees now summer's gone,
For fallen with their leaves are those glad days
Of sand and sea and ships, of swallows, lambs,
Of cricket teams, and walking long in woods.

Standing among the trees a shadow bends
And picks a cigarette-end from the ground;
It lifts the collar of an overcoat,
And blows upon its hands and stamps its feet—
For this is winter, chastiser of the free,
This is the winter, kind only to the bound.

Clifford Dyment

THE EMIGRANT

Going by Daly's shanty I heard the boys within
Dancing the Spanish hornpipe to Driscoll's violin,
I heard the sea-boots shaking the rough planks of the floor,
But I was going westward, I hadn't heart for more.

All down the windy village the noise rang in my ears,
Old sea-boots stamping, shuffling, it brought the bitter tears.
The old tune piped and quavered, the lilts came clear and
   strong,
But I was going westward, I couldn't join the song.

There were the grey stone houses, the night wind blowing keen,
The hill-sides pale with moonlight, the young corn springing
   green,
The hearth nooks lit and kindly, with dear friends good to see,
But I was going westward, and the ship waited me.

John Masefield

KINDNESS TO ANIMALS

Little children, never give
Pain to things that feel and live:
Let the gentle robin come
For the crumbs you save at home —
As his meat you throw along
He'll repay you with a song;
Never hurt the timid hare
Peeping from her green grass lair,
Let her come and sport and play
On the lawn at close of day;
The little lark goes soaring high
To the bright windows of the sky,
Singing as if 'twere always spring,
And fluttering on an untired wing —
Oh! let him sing his happy song,
Nor do these gentle creatures wrong.

Anon.

DOUBLE DUTCH

That crafty cat, a buff-black Siamese,
　　Sniffing through wild wood, sagely, silently goes,
Prick ears, lank legs, alertly twitching nose,
And on her secret errand reads with ease
　　A language no man knows.

Walter de la Mare

BADGER

When midnight comes a host of dogs and men
Go out and track the badger to his den,
And put a sack within the hole, and lie
Till the old grunting badger passes by.
He comes and hears—they let the strongest loose.
The old fox hears the noise and drops the goose.
The poacher shoots and hurries from the cry,
And the old hare half wounded buzzes by.
They get a forkèd stick to bear him down
And clap the dogs and take him to the town,
And bait him all the day with many dogs,
And laugh and shout and fright the scampering hogs.
He runs along and bites at all he meets:
They shout and hollo down the noisy streets . . .

from *Badger*, John Clare

SHEEP

When I was once in Baltimore
  A man came up to me and cried,
"Come, I have eighteen hundred sheep,
  And we will sail on Tuesday's tide.

"If you will sail with me, young man,
  I'll pay you fifty shillings down;
These eighteen hundred sheep I take
  From Baltimore to Glasgow town."

He paid me fifty shillings down,
  I sailed with eighteen hundred sheep;
We soon had cleared the harbour's mouth,
  We soon were in the salt sea deep.

The first night we were out at sea
  Those sheep were quiet in their mind;
The second night they cried with fear—
  They smelt no pastures in the wind.

They sniffed, poor things, for their green fields,
  They cried so loud I could not sleep:
For fifty thousand shillings down
  I would not sail again with sheep.

W. H. Davies

OLIPHAUNT

Grey as a mouse,
Big as a house,
Nose like a snake,
I make the earth shake,
As I tramp through the grass;
Trees crack as I pass.
With horns in my mouth
I walk in the South,
Flapping big ears.
Beyond count of years
I stump round and round,
Never lie on the ground,
Not even to die.
Oliphaunt am I,
Biggest of all,
Huge, old, and tall.
If ever you'd met me,
You wouldn't forget me.
If you never do,
You won't think I'm true;
But old Oliphaunt am I,
And I never lie.

J. R. R. Tolkien

FIDELITY

A barking sound the Shepherd hears,
A cry as of a dog or fox;
He halts—and searches with his eyes
Among the scattered rocks:
And now at distance can discern
A stirring in a brake of fern;
And instantly a dog is seen,
Glancing through that covert green.

The Dog is not of mountain breed;
Its motions, too, are wild and shy;
With something, as the Shepherd thinks,
Unusual in its cry:
Nor is there any one in sight
All round, in hollow or on height:
Nor shout, nor whistle strikes his ear;
What is the creature doing here?

It was a cove, a huge recess,
That keeps, till June, December's snow;
A lofty precipice in front,
A silent tarn below!
Far in the bosom of Helvellyn,
Remote from public road or dwelling,
Pathway, or cultivated land;
From trace of human foot or hand.

. . . . . .

Not free from boding thoughts, a while
The Shepherd stood; then makes his way
O'er rocks and stones, following the Dog
As quickly as he may;
Nor far had gone before he found
A human skeleton on the ground;
The appalled Discoverer with a sigh
Looks round, to learn the history.

From those abrupt and perilous rocks
The Man had fallen, that place of fear!
At length upon the Shepherd's mind
It breaks, and all is clear:
He instantly recalled the name,
And who he was, and whence he came;
Remembered, too, the very day
On which the Traveller passed this way.

But hear a wonder, for whose sake
This lamentable tale I tell!
A lasting monument of words
This wonder merits well.
The Dog, which still was hovering nigh,
Repeating the same timid cry,
This Dog, had been through three months' space
A dweller in that savage placc.

Yes, proof was plain that, since the day
When this ill-fated Traveller died,
The Dog had watched about the spot,
Or by his master's side;
How nourished here through such long time
He knows, who gave that love sublime;
And gave that strength of feeling, great
Above all human estimate!

from *Fidelity*, William Wordsworth

I HAVE A FAWN

I have a fawn from Aden's land,
On leafy buds and berries nursed;
And you shall feed him from your hand,
Though he may start with fear at first.
And I will lead you where he lies
For shelter in the noon-day heat:
And you may touch his sleeping eyes,
And feel his little silver feet.

Thomas Moore

THE HORSE OF ADONIS

Round-hoofed, short-jointed, fetlocks shag and long,
Broad breast, full eye, small head, and nostril wide,
High crest, short ears, straight legs, and passing strong,
Thin mane, thick tail, broad buttock, tender hide . . .
Sometimes he scuds far off, and there he stares;
Anon he starts at stirring of a feather;
To bid the wind a base* he now prepares,
And whe'r he run or fly they know not whether;
For through his mane and tail the high wind sings,
Fanning the hairs, who wave like feather'd wings.

from *Venus and Adonis*, William Shakespeare

* base; a country game

THE CHAMELEON

Two travellers of such a cast,
As o'er Arabia's wilds they passed,
And on their way, in friendly chat,
Now talked of this, and then of that;
Discoursed awhile, 'mongst other matter,
Of the chameleon's form and nature.
"A stranger animal," cries one,
"Sure never lived beneath the sun:
A lizard's body lean and long,
A fish's head, a serpent's tongue,
Its foot with triple claw disjoined;
And what a length of tail behind!
How slow its pace! and then its hue—
Who ever saw so fine a blue?"
    "Hold there," the other quick replies;
"'Tis green—I saw it with these eyes,
As late with open mouth it lay,
And warmed it in the sunny ray;
Stretched at its ease, the beast I viewed,
And saw it eat the air for food."
    "I've seen it, sir, as well as you,
And must again affirm it blue;
At leisure I the beast surveyed
Extended in the cooling shade."
    "'Tis green, 'tis green, sir, I assure ye."
"Green!" cries the other in a fury:
"Why, sir, d'ye think I've lost my eyes?"
"'Twere no great loss," the friend replies;
"For if they always serve you thus,
You'll find them but of little use."

So high at last the contest rose,
From words they almost came to blows:
When luckily came by a third;
To him the question they referred:
And begged he'd tell them, if he knew,
Whether the thing was green or blue.

  "Sirs," cries the umpire, "cease your pother;
The creature's neither one nor t'other.
I caught the animal last night,
And viewed it o'er by candlelight:
I marked it well; 'twas black as jet—
You stare—but, sirs, I've got it yet,
And can produce it."—"Pray, sir, do;
I'll lay my life the thing is blue."
"And I'll be sworn, that when you've seen
The reptile, you'll pronounce him green."

  "Well, then, at once to ease the doubt,"
Replies the man, "I'll turn him out:
And when before your eyes I've set him,
If you don't find him black, I'll eat him."

  He said; and full before their sight
Produced the beast, and lo!—'twas white.

from *The Chameleon*, James Merrick

WHEN THE ANIMALS WERE LET OUT
OF THE ARK AFTER THE FLOOD

There was scurrying and scrimmage when the wild ones
    all escaped:
Each fowl took to flight, that his feathers would serve,
Each fish to the flood that could use its fins,
Each beast to the fields that feeds on herbs,
Wild worms to their homes wriggle in the earth,
The fox and the pole-cat wend to the wood,
Harts to the high heath, hares to the gorse,
And lions and leopards to the lake-caverns,
Eagles and hawks to the high rocks,
The whole-footed fowl fares to the flood,
And each beast in a bustle to where best he likes.

14th Century

THE BOY FISHING

I am cold and alone,
On my tree-root sitting as still as stone.
The fish come to my net. I scorned the sun,
The voices on the road, and they have gone.
My eyes are buried in the cold pond, under
The cold, spread leaves; my thoughts are silver-wet.
I have ten stickleback, a half-day's plunder,
Safe in my jar. I shall have ten more yet.

E. J. Scovell

THE CREATION

    . . . there was no sun
To light the universe; there was no moon
With slender silver crescents filling slowly;
No earth hung balanced in surrounding air;
No sea reached far along the fringe of shore.
Land, to be sure, there was, and air, and ocean,
But land on which no man could stand, and water
No man could swim in, air no man could breathe,
Air without light . . .

    from *Metamorphoses*, Ovid
    Translated by Rolfe Humphries

RIDING TOGETHER

For many, many days together
   The wind blew steady from the East;
For many days, hot grew the weather,
   About the time of Our Lady's Feast.

For many days we rode together
   Yet met we neither friend nor foe;
Hotter and clearer grew the weather,
   Steadily did the East wind blow.

We saw the trees in the hot, bright weather,
   Clear-cut with shadows very black,
As freely we rode on together
   With helms unlaced and bridles slack.

And often as we rode together,
   We, looking down the green-banked stream,
Saw flowers in the sunny weather,
   And saw the bubble-making bream.

And in the night lay down together,
   And hung above our heads the rood,
Or watch'd night long in the dewy weather,
   The while the moon did watch the wood.

Our spears stood bright and thick together,
   Straight out the banners stream'd behind,
As we galloped on in the sunny weather,
   With faces turn'd towards the wind.

Down sank our threescore spears together,
　As thick we saw the pagans ride;
His eager face in the clear, fresh weather,
　Shone out that last time by my side.

Up the sweep of the bridge we dash'd together,
　It rock'd to the crash of the meeting spears,
Down rain'd the buds of the dear Spring weather,
　The elm tree flowers fell like tears.

There, as we roll'd and writhed together,
　I threw my arms above my head,
For close by my side in the lovely weather,
　I saw him reel and fall back dead.

I and the slayer met together,
　He waited the death-stroke there in his place,
With thoughts of death in the lovely weather,
　Gapingly mazed at my madden'd face.

Madly I fought as we fought together;
　In vain: the little Christian band
The pagans drowned, as in stormy weather,
　The river drowns low-lying land.

They bound my blood-stain'd hands together,
　They bound his corpse to nod by my side;
Then on we rode in the bright March weather,
　With clash of cymbals did we ride.

We ride no more, no more together;
    My prison bars are thick and strong,
I take no heed of any weather,
    The sweet saints grant I live not long.

William Morris

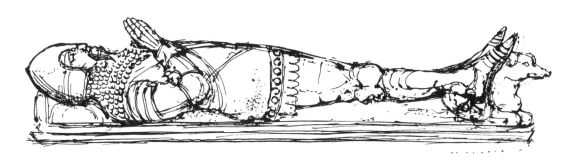

THE KNIGHT'S TOMB

Where is the grave of Sir Arthur O'Kellyn?
Where may the grave of that good man be?—
By the side of a spring, on the breast of Helvellyn,
Under the twigs of a young birch tree!
The oak that in summer was sweet to hear,
And rustled its leaves in the fall of the year,
And whistled and roared in the winter alone,
Is gone,—and the birch in its stead is grown.—
The Knight's bones are dust,
And his good sword rust;—
His soul is with the saints, I trust.

Samuel Taylor Coleridge

FLODDEN

But as they left the dark'ning heath,
More desperate grew the strife of death.
The English shafts in volleys hail'd,
In headlong charge their horse assail'd;
Front, flank, and rear, the squadrons sweep
To break the Scottish circle deep,
    That fought around their King.
But yet, though thick the shafts as snow,
Though charging knights like whirlwinds go,
Though bill-men ply the ghastly blow,
    Unbroken was the ring;
The stubborn spear-men still made good
Their dark impenetrable wood,
Each stepping where his comrade stood,
    The instant that he fell.
No thought was there of dastard flight;
Link'd in the serried phalanx tight,
Groom fought like noble, squire like knight,
    As fearlessly and well;
Till utter darkness closed her wing
O'er their thin host and wounded King.

from *Flodden*, Sir Walter Scott

THE DISCOVERY

There was an Indian, who had known no change,
   Who strayed content along a sunlit beach
Gathering shells. He heard a sudden strange
   Commingled noise: looked up; and gasped for speech.

For in the bay, where nothing was before,
   Moved on the sea, by magic, huge canoes,
With bellying cloths on poles, and not one oar,
   And fluttering coloured signs and clambering crews.

And he, in fear, this naked man alone,
   His fallen hands forgetting all their shells,
His lips gone pale, knelt low behind a stone,
   And stared, and saw, and did not understand,
   Columbus's doom-burdened caravels
     Slant to the shore, and all their seamen land.

J. C. Squire

THE MINSTREL BOY

The Minstrel Boy to the war is gone
   In the ranks of death you'll find him,
His father's sword he has girded on,
   And his wild harp slung behind him.

"Land of song!" said the warrior bard,
   "Tho' all the world betrays thee,
One sword, at least, thy rights shall guard,
   One faithful harp shall praise thee."

The minstrel fell! but the foeman's chain
   Could not bring that proud soul under;
The harp he loved ne'er spoke again,
   For he tore its chords asunder;
And said, "No chain shall sully thee,
   Thou soul of love and bravery.
Thy songs were made for the pure and free,
   They shall never sound in slavery."

Thomas Moore

LORD RANDAL

"O where hae ye been, Lord Randal, my son?
O where hae ye been, my handsome young man?"—
"I hae been to the wild wood; mother, make my bed soon,
For I'm weary wi' hunting, and fain wald lie down."

"Where gat ye your dinner, Lord Randal, my son?
Where gat ye your dinner, my handsome young man?"—
"I dined wi' my true-love; mother, make my bed soon,
For I'm weary wi' hunting, and fain wald lie down."

"What gat ye to your dinner, Lord Randal, my son?
What gat ye to your dinner, my handsome young man?"—
"I gat eels boil'd in broo'; mother, make my bed soon,
For I'm weary wi' hunting, and fain wald lie down."

"What became of your bloodhounds, Lord Randal, my son?
What became of your bloodhounds, my handsome young
    man?"—
"O they swell'd and they died; mother, make my bed soon,
For I'm weary wi' hunting, and fain wald lie down."

"O I fear ye are poison'd, Lord Randal, my son!
O I fear ye are poison'd, my handsome young man!"—
"O yes! I am poison'd; mother, make my bed soon,
For I'm sick at the heart, and I fain wald lie down."

Anon.

MEG MERRILIES

Old Meg she was a Gipsy,
　　And liv'd upon the Moors:
Her bed it was the brown heath turf,
　　And her house was out of doors.

Her apples were swart blackberries,
　　Her currants pods o' broom;
Her wine was dew of the wild white rose,
　　Her book a churchyard tomb.

Her Brothers were the craggy hills,
　　Her Sisters larchen trees;
Alone with her great family
　　She liv'd as she did please.

No breakfast had she many a morn,
　　No dinner many a noon,
And 'stead of supper she would stare
　　Full hard against the Moon.

But every morn of woodbine fresh
　　She made her garlanding,
And every night the dark glen Yew
　　She wove, and she would sing.

And with her fingers old and brown,
　　She plaited Mats o' Rushes,
And gave them to the Cottagers
　　She met among the Bushes.

Old Meg was brave as Margaret Queen,
    And tall as Amazon;
An old red blanket cloak she wore,
    A chip hat had she on:
God rest her agèd bones somewhere—
    She died full long agone!

John Keats

THE DISMANTLED SHIP

In some unused lagoon, some nameless bay,
On sluggish, lonesome waters, anchor'd near the shore,
An old, dismasted, gray and batter'd ship, disabled, done,
After free voyages to all the seas of earth, haul'd up
    at last and hawser'd tight,
Lies rusting, mouldering.

Walt Whitman

THE SANDS OF DEE

"O Mary, go and call the cattle home,
      And call the cattle home,
      And call the cattle home,
      Across the sands of Dee!"
The western wind was wild and dank with foam,
      And all alone went she.

The western tide crept up along the sand,
      And o'er and o'er the sand,
      And round and round the sand,
      As far as eye could see.
The rolling mist came down and hid the land:
      And never home came she.

"O is it weed, or fish, or floating hair—
      A tress of golden hair,
      A drowned maiden's hair,
      Above the nets at sea?"
Was never salmon yet that shone so fair,
      Among the stakes of Dee.

They rowed her in across the rolling foam,
      The cruel crawling foam,
      The cruel hungry foam,
      To her grave beside the sea;
But still the boatmen hear her call the cattle home,
      Across the sands of Dee.

Charles Kingsley

AT CHRISTMAS

I wish you a Merry Christmas,
I wish you a Merry Christmas,
I wish you a Merry Christmas
And a Happy New Year.

Good tidings I bring
To you and your kin;
I wish you a Merry Christmas
And a Happy New Year.

Now bring us some figgy pudding,
Now bring us some figgy pudding,
Now bring us some figgy pudding,
And bring some out here.

For we all like figgy pudding,
We all like figgy pudding,
For we all like figgy pudding,
So bring some out here.

And we won't go till we've got some,
And we won't go till we've got some,
And we won't go till we've got some,
So bring some out here.

Good tidings I bring
To you and your kin;
I wish you a Merry Christmas
And a Happy New Year.

Anon.

HOT CAKE

Winter has come; fierce is the cold;
In the sharp morning air new-risen we meet.
Rheum freezes in the nose;
Frost hangs about the chin.
For hollow bellies, for chattering teeth and
      shivering knees
What better than hot cake?
Soft as the down of spring,
Whiter than autumn floss!
Dense and swift the steam
Rises, swells and spreads.
Fragrance flies through the air,
Is scattered far and wide,
Steals down along the wind and wets
The covetous mouth of passer-by.

Servants and grooms
Throw sidelong glances, munch the empty air.
They lick their lips who serve;
While lines of envious lackeys by the wall
Stand dryly swallowing.

from *Hot Cake*, Shu Hsi, *c.* A.D. 265–306
Translated by Arthur Waley

AN OLD GRACE

God bless our meat,
God guide our ways,
God give us grace
Our Lord to please.
Lord, long preserve in peace and health
Our gracious Queen Elizabeth.

Anon.

CHRISTMAS TIME

The fire, with well-dried logs supplied,
Went roaring up the chimney wide;
The huge hall-table's oaken face,
Scrubbed till it shone the day to grace,
Bore then upon its massive board
No mark to part the squire and lord.
Then was brought in the lusty brawn,
By old blue-coated serving-man;
Then the grim boar's head frowned on high,
Crested with bays and rosemary.
Well can the green-garbed ranger tell,
How, when, and where, the monster fell:
What dogs before his death he tore,
And all the baiting of the boar.
The wassel round in good brown bowls,
Garnished with ribbons, blithely trowls.

There the huge sirloin reeked; hard by
Plum-porridge stood, and Christmas pie
Nor failed old Scotland to produce,
At such high-tide, her savoury goose.

from *Christmas Time*, Sir Walter Scott

A RHYME FOR
SHROVE TUESDAY

Snick, snock, the pan's hot,
We be come a-shrovin'.
Please to gie us summat,
Summat's better'n nothin':
A bit o' bread, a bit o' cheese,
A bit o' apple dumplin' please.

Anon.

PANCAKES

Mix a pancake,
Stir a pancake,
   Pop it in the pan;
Fry the pancake,
Toss the pancake,—
   Catch it if you can.

Christina Rossetti

BRING US IN GOOD ALE

Bring us in no brown bread for that is made of bran,
Nor bring us in no white bread for therein is no gain,
But bring us in good ale.

Bring us in no beef for there is many bones,
But bring us in good ale. For that goes down at once.
And bring us in good ale.

Bring us in no bacon for that is passing fat,
And bring us in good ale, and give us enough of that.
And bring us in good ale.

Bring us in no mutton, for that is often lean,
And bring us in no tripes, for they be seldom clean.
And bring us in good ale.

Bring us in no eggys for there are many shells,
But bring us in good ale, and bring us nothing else.
And bring us in good ale.

Bring us in no butter for therein are many hairs,
And bring us in no pig's flesh for that will make us bears.
And bring us in good ale.

Bring us in no puddings for therein is all God's good,
Nor bring us in no venison, for that is not for our blood.
But bring us in good ale.

Bring us in no capon's flesh for that is often dear,
Nor bring us in no duck's flesh for they slobber in the mere.
But bring us in good ale.

Anon.

Nose, nose, jolly red nose,
And who gave thee this jolly red nose?
Nutmegs and ginger, cinnamon and cloves,
And they gave me this jolly red nose.

Beaumont and Fletcher

BUSY, CURIOUS, THIRSTY FLY

Busy, curious, thirsty fly,
Drink with me, and drink as I;
Freely welcome to my cup,
Couldst thou sip, and sip it up.
Make the most of life you may;
Life is short, and wears away.

Both alike are mine and thine,
Hastening quick to their decline;
Thine's a summer, mine's no more,
Though repeated to threescore!
Threescore summer, when they're gone,
Will appear as short as one.

Anon.

TURTLE SOUP

Beautiful Soup, so rich and green,
Waiting in a hot tureen!
Who for such dainties would not stoop?
Soup of the evening, beautiful Soup!
Soup of the evening, beautiful Soup!
    Beau-ootiful Soo-oop!
    Beau-ootiful Soo-oop!
Soo-oop of the e-e-evening,
    Beautiful, beautiful Soup.

Beautiful Soup! Who cares for fish,
Game, or any other dish?
Who would not give all else for two p-
ennyworth only of beautiful Soup?
Pennyworth only of beautiful Soup?
    Beau-ootiful Soo-oop!
    Beau-ootiful Soo-oop!
Soo-oop of the e-e-evening,
    Beautiful, beauti-FUL SOUP!

      Lewis Carroll

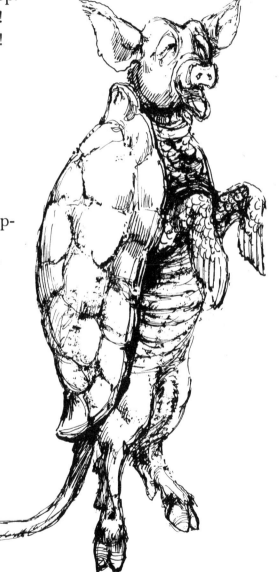

INDEX OF FIRST LINES

INDEX OF FIRST LINES

[101]

INDEX OF FIRST LINES

INDEX OF AUTHORS

ACKNOWLEDGMENTS

The publishers have made every effort to trace the ownership of the copyright material in this book. It is their belief that the necessary permissions from publishers, authors and authorised agents have been obtained, but in the event of any question arising as to the use of any material, the publishers, while expressing regret for any error unconsciously made, will be pleased to make the necessary correction in future editions of this book.

George Allen & Unwin Ltd for 'Summer' by Richard Aldington, 'Oliphaunt' by J. R. R. Tolkien from *Tom Bombadil*, 'Hot Cake' by Shu Hsi, translated by Arthur Waley; Mrs Gwyneth Redwood-Anderson and Macdonald & Co. (Publishers) Ltd for 'Jardins sous la Pluie' by John Redwood-Anderson from *Almanac*; Blackie & Son Ltd for 'Who's in?' by Elizabeth Fleming from *In Poem Town—Book I*; Constable & Co. Ltd for 'Spanish Folk Song' translated by S. De Madariaga; The Cresset Press Ltd for 'Cambridge' by Frances Cornford and 'The Boy Fishing' by E. J. Scovell; Mrs H. M. Davies, Jonathan Cape Ltd, London and the Wesleyan University Press, Middleton, Connecticut for 'Sheep' from *The Complete Poems of W. H. Davies*; the Literary Trustees of Walter de la Mare and The Society of Authors as their representative for 'The Pool in the Rock' and 'Double Dutch' by Walter de la Mare; J. M. Dent & Sons Ltd for 'The Winter Trees' by Clifford Dyment from *The Axe in the Wood*; Gerald Duckworth & Co. Ltd for 'Winter the Huntsman' by Osbert Sitwell from *Selected Poems Old and New*; Mr Michael Gibson and Macmillan & Co. Ltd for 'The Wind and the Rain' by W. W. Gibson from *The Golden Room and Other Poems*; the Author for 'Wander-Thirst' by Gerald Gould from *The Golden Staircase* compiled by Louey Chisholm; Rupert Hart-Davis for 'Snow Harvest' by Andrew Young from *Collected Poems*; Indiana University Press for Ovid's *Metamorphoses*, translated by Rolfe Humphries; the Literary Estate of F. L. Lucas and The Hogarth Press Ltd for 'Beleaguered Cities' by F. L. Lucas from *Time and Memory* (1929); the Author for 'Evening Over the Forest' by Beatrice Mayor from *An Approach to Modern Poetry*, edited by Teskey & Parker; Mrs D. M. Mewton-Wood for 'Romance' by W. J. Turner from *Collected Poems*; the Estate of the late Edna St. Vincent Millay for 'Afternoon on a Hill' from *The Golden Staircase* compiled by Louey Chisholm; Methuen & Co. Ltd for 'Old Dan'l' by L. A. G. Strong from *The Body's Imperfection*; the Author for 'Town and Country' by Thomas Moult; Laurence Pollinger Ltd, London, the Estate of the late Mrs Frieda Lawrence and The Viking Press Inc., New York for 'Talk' from *The Complete Poems of D. H. Lawrence, Volume I*, edited by Vivian de Sola Pinto and F. Warren Roberts, Copyright © 1929 by Frieda Lawrence Ravagli, all rights reserved; the late Siegfried Sassoon for 'Noah' from *Collected Poems*; Mr Raglan Squire and Macmillan & Co. Ltd for 'The Discovery' by J. C. Squire from *Collected Poems*; The Society of Authors as the Literary Representative of the Estate of the late Dr John Masefield, O.M. and The Macmillan Company, New York for 'Trade Winds' and 'The Emigrant' by John Masefield from *Collected Poems*, Copyright © for 'Trade Winds' 1916 by John Masefield, renewed 1944 by John Masefield, Copyright © for 'The Emigrant' 1912 by The Macmillan Company, renewed 1940 by John Masefield; The Society of Authors as the Literary Representative of the Estate of the late James Stephens for 'The Hill of Vision' by James Stephens; Mrs Iris Wise, Macmillan & Co. Ltd, London and The Macmillan Company, New York for 'And it was Windy Weather' by James Stephens from *Collected Poems*, Copyright © 1915 by The Macmillan Company, renewed 1943 by James Stephens.